this book is not for sale
and you'd be a fool to buy it

stories

Jeremy Bronaugh

Hypertrophic Press

"Passion Fruit" first appeared in *Black Fox Literary*.
"Salesmanship" first appeared in *The Southern Tablet*.
"Summer Sleep" first appeared in *The Southern Tablet*.

ISBN-13: 978-0692314791
ISBN-10: 0692314792

Hypertrophic Press
P.O. Box 423, New Market, AL, 35761
www.hypertrophicpress.com

For you, who chose to read this when you could be
watching *Law and Order*.

stories

this book is not for sale
and you'd be a fool to buy it

disappointment

You're eight years old and you and your little brother are playing with action figures. Wolverine and
Deadpool slash at each other with their retractable
claws and knife respectively, but you know, and
your little brother does too – you think – that no
harm can really come to either of them. This can go
on forever; they have healing factors.

It's time to pack it up, who knows why – maybe
Mom's calling for dinner or maybe you're just bored
of bashing a yellow plastic man into a red plastic

man. Or maybe you're learning already to hate being around your brother, although you doubt that because he wasn't always like he is now. But anyway, you're packing your shit up and you get the bright idea to transfer the toys faster by tossing them down from the third floor to the second instead of carrying them.

It would have been faster to carry them, but don't be too hard on yourself, you were eight.

So your baby brother stays up on the third floor and drops the toys down to you through the railing. He drops Wolverine and you catch him. Cable. Stryfe. Nightcrawler. Then he gets ready to hand off his favorite, the red modeled plastic grail – Deadpool.

You'll catch him, you promise. You swear.

But you don't.

And Deadpool shatters against the hardwood floor, sending shards of red plastic debris scattering at your feet. You didn't catch him. His eyes, your brother's, you see them go wide. This might be the first time you ever let someone down. You don't know. You're eight.

summer sleep

Dime-sized frogs sprouted by the hundreds at my shitty apartment – in the yard, on my window, all over my porch. They were near impossible to avoid as I tiptoed to my car, a delicate dance intended to evade their erratic jumping.

Scratch that. They were impossible to avoid.

I stepped on the largest one I'd seen that week-end. Even with its organs blooming on the pavement, its legs hanging limp and lifeless, it was only the size of a quarter.

Its chest filled and released, each breath taken in vain.

I carried it inside, carefully cradling it in my palm, and put it in a Ziploc bag, hoping to asphyxiate it, to send it off without further trauma.

But his breaths still came in, shallow and defiant. His eyelids flitted over his tiny, glass eyes.

I waited, hoping it would end quickly.

But it didn't.

Each breath was an accusation. And I, knowing that I had already killed him, put the bag under my tire and drove away.

passion fruit

I'm maybe three drinks in when I decide it's a good idea to cover my hand in Bacardi 151 and light it on fire.

I let the flame lick my fingers before I shake it out. The group looks at me, half vexed and half awed, like I invented fire. Someone offers me a shot. It's hard to tell each face apart, so the names get lost. But this guy is handing me a shot and I take it from him, set it on fire, then blow on it and pour it into my mouth.

He's impressed, but I've done this trick already, played with fire. He sits back down at the table with some other faces. I walk into the kitchen to wash the rum residue off and see Claire leaning against the sink like she's about to throw up. Claire, the consummate hostess. We're all in her apartment, maybe fifteen of us in something like twelve hundred square feet. I'm guessing she has anxiety issues because she is flat-out, stupid drunk. I pull a light beer from the fridge, crack it, and set my hand on her shoulder.

"Nice turnout," I say.

She bites my hand. Not like play bites, but actually fucking bites me. Breaks the skin even, and little bubbles of blood form in her vampire kiss.

"What the fuck's that about?" I say, running my hand under water.

"You're a dick," she says, and she waltzes into her living room.

I step outside to smoke, rubbing the space between my thumb and index finger, raised and swollen from the bite, singed a little from playing Human Torch. A girl is leaning over the railing, the kind of girl you notice right away. She turns to see who invaded her space. Black hair and blue eyes. Wide smile and soft features. The reason someone first said the word beautiful.

"Hello," she says in a tight, Slavic accent. Foreign but clear.

"Hey," I say, offering her a cigarette. She pulls one from the pack with thin, delicate fingers and I light it. She leans back against the railing, smoke pluming up from her lips, and I flick the lighter again, lighting my own cigarette, a tiny bar to measure the conversation. I have exactly one cigarette's length to talk to this girl without looking like an ass.

"It's too loud in there," I say, nodding toward the glass door that partitions the rest of the world from the warm summer night.

"Says the boy who lights himself on fire." She slides toward me and, cigarette in mouth, takes my hand in hers to inspect it. "It does not hurt?"

I open and close my hand, move each finger, and answer. "The flame never touches my skin. Just burns up the alcohol."

She takes a long drag and lets it out in a measured breath, careful to expel only as much air as smoke. "So you are in need of attention then?"

I smile, busted. Her cigarette burns down, and she ashes it.

"It is–" she starts, but is interrupted by the sliding glass door.

"We're gonna make a trip to the gas station 'fore it closes," Claire says. "Did ya'll want anything?"

"We will also go," the girl says, and I realize I don't know her name.

The gas station is maybe four blocks away, like a quarter mile. A whole, dumb group pours out from the party and reforms into a little posse of drunks stumbling across streets and parking lots into the night. This guy, about half my size, keeps talking about his side job as a Spider-Man impersonator, but I have to force myself to listen to him instead of looking at the Slavic girl. She moves like she looks, beautiful in tight jeans and a black t-shirt. Nothing out of place but her.

I side-step to Claire. "Who's the Russian?"

She scans the group, like it's full of Russians and she needs clarification, then turns back to me and says, "Why? Do you like her?"

"Just tell me her name."

"And if I don't want to?" she asks, half stumbling to keep pace and look at me at the same time.

I growl under my breath, but Claire catches it and I know I made a mistake. She turns to mock me, walking backwards as she says, "Somebody got a crush?"

"If you aren't going to tell me–"

Claire trips and falls backwards. I grab her hands and catch her just before she hits the pavement.

"Helina," she says in a sober moment, then starts laughing, quiet at first and then uncontrollable. I duck out.

In the parking lot of a super center, only a minute or so from the gas station, we come across a closed-up fruit stand, a mountain of watermelon encased by wooden walls and guarded by a metal, latticed fence that's padlocked at one end.

"It would be so nice to have a watermelon," Helina says, eyeballing the stand with sincerity.

"Maybe they'll have some at the gas station," I

say, because sometimes little gas stations have shit you wouldn't expect.

But not this one.

We step into the stark, fluorescent light, killing the ambient mystery of the night. I grab a six-pack of beer and scan for a watermelon, which they don't have, so I ask the cashier, "Do you have watermelons and I'm just not seeing them?"

"We have bananas," he says.

Yeah. Same thing, asshole. I pay for the beer and leave. Eventually so does everyone else and we start the trek back to Claire's apartment, back across the empty super store parking lot, and back to the fruit stand.

The stand is maybe five feet by five feet. Seven feet tall. The roof is diagonal, leaving enough space that a watermelon might fit through.

"Hold this," I say, handing the beer to Helina.

The group stops walking as I tighten my fingers and stick my hand through one of the holes in the gate. I roll a watermelon against the metal and palm it. Push it against the gate to steady it.

I lift it the length of my fingers, then use my

other hand to repeat, lifting it another few inches. I repeat this, over and over, raising the watermelon with one hand, then sticking my other hand into another slot in the fence, trading off and raising it another few inches. At six feet four inches, I'm just tall enough to reach the watermelon to the top, where I have to push with my fingertips to propel it over the gate.

It falls, and I catch it against my chest with both hands. The group cheers, apparently having held their breath in anticipation. Helina hugs my arm and says, "My hero."

"We should get out of here," I say, guilty of grand theft fruit, and we walk back to the apartment complex. Claire shoots me a look as the group walks up the stairs to her place, then scoffs and disappears into her apartment. Helina and I hang back, take a seat in the grass, and I use my pocket knife to cut big, ugly chunks out of the watermelon, handing every other piece to her.

I open two of the beers, hand one to her, and we clink them together.

"*Na zdorovya*," I say, and I'm drunk enough to

pull it off. To say it without a hint of embarrassment. I don't mention that's the only Russian I know, that I learned it watching a movie, that I'm only cultured by accident.

"You are a sweet boy," she says and wraps her watermelon-sticky fingers in mine.

They used to say the vein in your left ring finger runs directly to your heart. Vena amoris, it's called. But that's bullshit. All of the veins in your fingers, each and every one of them, run directly to your heart.

You'll be out of college about six months before you're desperate enough to take a commission sales job. They'll respond the same day you send in your resume and you'll have a meeting the next and the secretary will compliment everyone who walks in the door the same way. "That's a smart shirt-and-tie combo." Or "I love your dress." Or "What a cool purse."

Everything about it will feel too easy, but you don't know any better because this is your first job interview out of college. And when you interview and your would-be boss tells you the next step in the interview process is a full day of unpaid training you'll stop and question it, but you'll cave because what's your time worth, really?

You'll wear the same suit to the follow-up interview because you can't afford to pick up your dry cleaning, but the guy who interviews you this time, he's a team lead, not the main man like before, and he tells you you're going out in the field, out on sales, and this is something you wish you knew before you wore your good shoes, but you didn't, and when you get in his car you don't mention the stale pot smell and you don't pick the radio station because you're trying to make a good impression.

You'll be halfway from Louisville to Frankfurt, about an hour out, and your trainer will stop for breakfast. This is a ritual for him, you can tell, because the locals all know his name. He greets them all with his shit-eating smile before you're both seated and he asks if you want anything for breakfast. You're starving, but it isn't worth ordering in case he expects you to pay. So you watch him eat while he goes through his catalogue, tells you he makes $4000 a week, tells you how you too, if you have enough hustle, if you want it bad enough, can be like him.

You, sitting across the table drinking ice water, you do want to make $4000 a week. You do want to be like him.

You tell him you have the hustle.

You tell him you can make the sale.

So he says he's taking you out to one of his top clients. He's going to see if you've got it in you to sell sell sell. And on the way there red and blue light up the rearview mirror. This shit-eating salesman tells you it's nothing. He tells you it's some kind of mistake.

He wasn't speeding. You checked.

You hear the cop yell "Get out of the car!" as he walks over. Your interviewer, he gets out and closes the door. He's talking non-stop until the cop slams him against the hood and cuffs him, and then the cop starts to drag him away, only he stops to let your trainer tell you that you have to drive his car back to Louisville.

And then they're both gone. They're gone and you're stranded on the side of the road. When you get in the driver's side you realize that you don't know the way home, and that there's not enough gas even if you did.

But you start driving back anyway, because what else do you do? College didn't prepare you for the workforce. College didn't teach you to stop at the first gas station to memorize a map back, or to dig through his car for change. College didn't teach you that the pay stub you find in his glove box – the one that says he made $170 working in the last two weeks – means that he's full of shit.

When you pump the seven dollars of change you find into the gas tank, you throw the cashed roaches and loose weed you find in his car away too. You're careful on the way back, sitting in your suit and tie in a car that smells like pot and resentment, and you're sullen when you hand the keys over to the secretary back at the office, the one who compliments you again for the same shirt-and-tie combo you wore to the first interview.

borrowing

One of things they don't tell you when you work at a blood bank, that you have to learn for yourself, is that so much blood is diseased. So many people, walking around, picking up coffee, going about their lives, have Hepatitis B, or HIV, or occasionally even West Nile virus.

They don't talk about it, don't ever say much, but the 'contaminated' refrigerator keeps filling up. The whole place is full of fridges with glass doors. Hundreds of people donate each day, and every day ten or so bags of blood make it into the contaminated fridge – ten people who didn't know they had Hepatitis C, didn't know they had Syphilis, didn't know they had a Chagas parasite crawling around in their blood.

And worst of all: the company only tests for those six.

What they don't teach you, working at a blood bank, something you just pick up on your own: don't ever get a blood transfusion.

Because when that stranger saves your life, when the doctor pumps you full of liquid 1-Up, you are gaining a history. Cytomegalovirus, TTV, malaria, Toxoplasmosis, Lyme disease, HGV – fucking Hepatitis G – these are your friends now. If your donor led a wild life, now so have you.

And no one's going to mention it.

When You Bleed to Death

CHAPTER ONE

"Do you know what you're doing, Brody?" James asks.

He tenses his mouth to say something else, but doesn't.

I lean against the porch steps as he slips his hand into his bag and produces a 20-oz. Vanilla Coke bottle that he's filled with Dextromethorphan. DXM. I catch my reflection in the rose lenses of his sunglasses and realize that I haven't given his question much thought.

Before today, I've never done drugs.

"An over-the-counter bottle of Robitussin DM has enough DXM to take an average person to the first plateau." He explains a series of plateaus – levels of consciousness that '60s-era hippies achieved with DXM – each more intense than the last. According to James, DXM users have reported being abducted by aliens and melting into the sun and meeting God. I don't want to cut him off, but I'm not really listening. "This," he stops, choosing his words carefully, "this batch is as strong as it gets."

I reach out and he hands me the bottle.

"You seriously look like shit. When was the last time you ate?"

I haven't eaten since she died. Over a week ago. As I unscrew the cap, a putrid wave of chemical stench washes over me.

"This is the most rancid shit I've ever smelled," I say.

"You really don't have to take it. I'm worried about how you're going to react, you know, with how you feel."

I roll the bottle in my hands and envision James in his mom's kitchen, huddled over the stove in his sunglasses and a "Kiss the Cook" apron, pouring lighter fluid and ammonia into a bubbling pot of cough syrup. He sprinkles glittering pixie dust into the pot. The guaifenesin separates. He ladles it out. The pot simmers. The ammonia evaporates. He wipes the condensation from his glasses, carefully pours his work through a funnel, and – poof – he's sitting on my porch with enough liquid hallucination for me to see my dead girlfriend.

"You didn't answer me," he says. "Do you know what you're doing?"

I think about why I called James; I think about Valerie. Her robin's egg eyes sparkle like springtime, and just as quickly the memory fades.

"We'll see," I say before I choke down the whole bottle, stopping to gag at least twice. Gasoline couldn't taste any worse.

I throw up, but catch it in my mouth and swallow it.

"You've got about forty-five minutes before you're going to feel disconnected," James says. "They call it robo-tripping for a reason." He suddenly remembers to ask, "Are you on any prescription anti-histamines?"

I shake my head.

"The drug interaction would make your eyes bleed," he says.

I sigh and taste the lighter fluid in the soda. "Thanks, James," I say and stand up to walk into my house.

"Brody. This wasn't your fault."

I look back at him and nod as I close the door. Through my window I watch James back out of the driveway, watch his shit car disappear, and I pull the shades to drown the morning light.

I notice a dried smear of blood on the sheets as I pull my blanket aside to lie on my bed and wait for her. The awful taste of DXM lingers in my mouth.

An LCD clock glows on my dresser next to a framed picture of Valerie. Her smile lights up her cheeks. I watch as the numbers change, counting the minutes until I'll see her again.

The numbers begin to slowly melt from the clock's display, dripping onto the dresser. I run my hand over the length of my face as I watch. Holding my bottom lip against my chin with my middle finger, I glide the tip of my index finger over a row of teeth I find hidden in my mouth. The longer I spend fingering the bucket of teeth, the more I smell lighter fluid and I don't like the smell, so I stop.

Everything itches.

I stand up and smash the glass in the frame. The

sound echoes and I worry that it could wake my mother, who's still sleeping upstairs. I stand motionless, waiting for the sound of creaking floorboards or footsteps.

When I'm satisfied she didn't hear it, I carefully pull the shards of glass from the frame. A piece slips from my hand and cuts my thumb, covering it in slick, greasy blood. My fingers are longer than usual, and I struggle to use them to peel Valerie out of the frame. I stare into the photo and for a second I remember what it had been like to smell her skin.

At Valerie's wake I saw this guy from school, Jason. He was interning at the funeral home over the summer and he was there when the fire department brought her in. I caught him before the wake and asked him to open her coffin.

Jason looked at me for a long time before he said, "She was so messed up when she got here, Brody. It was gruesome." When I didn't say anything, he added, "You don't want to see her like that."

"I need to," I said, and he opened it.

She looked like a mannequin covered in latex skin and an old woman's makeup. I wanted to kiss her, but couldn't bring myself to touch the lifeless body.

I turn her photo over in my hands and see that a small pool of blood has formed in my palm. I set the photo down, accidentally dragging my bloody fingers across her face.

At the burial some stranger told me, "I hear it was a pretty bad wreck. There's no pain when the neck snaps like that." Like he would know.

I slide the glass fragments into my sock drawer, keeping the biggest shard. I close my fist around it until blood leaks through my fingers. I squeeze until the telephone rings, distracting me, and I set the bloody shard next to Valerie.

The ring echoes and I can feel it touch my skin.

I lift the receiver away from my ear and bite hard into my bottom lip as a chorus of voices asks, "How are you holding up?" Other voices tell me how sorry they are. Some of the voices sound familiar. Some of the voices cry.

"Are you there?" the voices ask. "Are you okay?"

They all get the same sobbing word-salad, the same lifeless robotic babble. They say things like "I'm so sorry" and "I'm here for you" and "It will be okay."

Blood trails down my hand and drips onto the mouthpiece of the phone.

I watch myself talking in the mirror. My eyes are

swollen. My hair is matted and wild. Water drips from my face and I realize that I'm crying.

I ask the voices what time it is. When they don't answer, I tell them Broderick isn't available and hang up.

Suddenly the light through the window blinds is excruciating. I open them and see that the world has dissolved into a painful white light.

It pulsates and tells me, "You are alone."

The phone rings again. I cough and lighter fluid rises in my throat, but the phone keeps ringing so I unplug it from the wall.

I have to find her. I did this to find her.

I dive into the ocean of my burgundy comforter and swim deep into the darkness of cream-colored sheets. The bubbles that escape my mouth rise slowly to the top of the ocean and make a familiar sound: Valerie.

My blood clouds the water so I swim deeper, pushing my arms through the resistance, feeling it spread through my fingers.

From the abyss, an ancient predator emerges like a biblical leviathan. The voids of its eyes are set against the colorless bone scales of its face. It could engulf me, tear me into strips of meat against its jagged teeth. I kick wildly, pushing out with frantic strokes. I push as hard as I am able, but it follows at my heels. Exhausted, I gasp for air and water fills my mouth. With a final gasp, I turn and reach out toward the monster.

His hollow eyes follow me as I descend into the void. I sink until his eyes fade.

In the depths of the black and unwelcoming ocean, as with everywhere else lately,

I find nothing.

This story is continued in
When You Bleed to Death: A Novel
Available on Amazon.com

Thank you.